The Story of the Paper Crown

JÓZEF CZECHOWICZ

The Story of the Paper Crown

Translated from the Polish by Frank Garrett

an object by
SUBLUNARY EDITIONS
of Seattle, WA

Originally published as "Opowieść o papierowej koronie" in *Reflektor*, 1923.

Translation copyright © 2023 Frank Garrett

ISBN 978–1–955190–61–9
LCCN 2023939755

Designed, printed, and bound in the greater Seattle area

Wholesale available at asterismbooks.com

Design and typesetting by Joshua Rothes

Typeset in Linotype Sabon Next and Din Pro. The cover font takes inspiration from Półtawski's Antiqua, an iconic antique typeface designed by Adam Półtawski between 1923 and 1928. It was designed specifically for the Polish language.

CONTENTS

EHEV fugaces, Postume, Postume,
labuntur anni nec pietas moram
rugis et instanti senectae
adferet indomitaeque morti…

WOE, Postumus, Postumus, the fleeting
years fly past, not even loyalty will delay
the wrinkles and pressing advance of dotage,
of predacious death…

— HORACE

You tell me my life story and things that will happen,
O black-eyed fortune teller hunched over your cards.
O dainty palms, my boyish future completely spun,
You are clear and profound in your straightforward words.

You're telling me my life story whilst the music thrums
And cries its pining waltz on a silver violin.
Today we're merry, and yet we're still so full of gloom
Like a winter day… Like kids left alone in their crib.

You tell me my story, but I'm listening to some whoosh
That trees outside the window swoosh in the autumn rain.
My soul sings again… In solitude or in a crowd
When it hears itself, it's fun and games, it sobs and sings.

Since today's a holiday, it plays like a violin,
And the Truth appears before my eyes—ever more plainly
That throughout this evening of fortune-telling
our strange friendship's starry yarn spins my smiling fate.

THE STORY OF THE PAPER CROWN

PROLOGUE

Fickle is the human soul, in which destructions and creations swirl while colorful spring months pass by in a procession of sunny days.

July—the middle of summer.

Dawn rises from the mists, and the gray half-light stretches across the quiet chamber. The night's debate continues. Henryk, standing by the window, is speaking, gazing at beds of poppies in bloom, speaking as if to the breaking dawn instead of the people who are listening to him.

"You say that fate exists. You believe in this bogeyman with all the faith of deeply convinced souls. But I—I do not know how to believe in that which indiscriminately happens by chance. If that were the case, I would be too much like the people for whom the tragedy of guilt and punishment is the greatest tragedy of all.

"Przybyszewski believed in random chance because he believed in the consequences of guilt. He said that there is punishment, but that there's no such thing as guilt. Oh, he still believed that guilt exists; it's just that he absolved himself of it, and he sorely lamented the disparity of these moments.

"Even if we are struck by this uneven, discordant, involuntary creative force, this exaggeration of punishment, then we must still put it on our own shoulders and not on the shoulders of fate. We alone create guilt and punishment. And the inexorability of this consequence lies within ourselves..."

At this, Father Clarus shifted nervously, sinking down into the pile of soft rugs and furs tossed in the corner.

"Master," he declared, "I love your soul with my whole heart but I do not love your words. They are different from you. In the evening when the moon rises over the hills, do you not feel that He exists? A compulsion within ourselves, you say. Why does it not come from outside? From Him?"

Henryk's slight smile was visible. His three friends stared at him in silence. All night they had talked together while he looked at the stars, and now that the stars had faded, he alone spoke.

"How in the world can you talk about something from the outside when nothing from the outside ever reaches us? Every soul is alone and cut off from the rest of the world. Every soul has only itself and lives on its own—in and of itself. If it is miry clay, then its life is miry clay. But sometimes it's irradiant, and sometimes it's a distant brightness, and sometimes, a titanic terror. There are also souls that Dionysian frenzy and tranquil Apollinian beauty wrench back and forth. Each of us is all alone, like a diver at the bottom of the sea. And you talk of external influences. We are oblivious to such things..."

When he fell silent, something terrible and anxious stirred in the three souls.

In his mind, Father Clarus kept repeating, "Each of us is solitary and alone..."

Postumus Porco, the one who always regarded Henryk skeptically, was lost deep in thought. Beneath his furrowed brow the labor of difficult, logical thought was suddenly felt. —Mental capacity was appraised there like precise mathematical values. This latest pronouncement didn't quite measure up.

But nearby, in Zygmunt's wide blue eyes a sadness glimmered, bearing witness to the truth. This one was indeed always alone, with the melancholic beauty of his own life. A babe of the fields on city pavement.

Once more Henryk's faint voice, lost in the poppy fragrance wafting from the garden along with the morning damp.

"The sun?

"Not yet. Only a glimmer, merely the predawn turning golden in the clear sky.

"... There's a strange beauty in a casual dream under little apple trees full of fruit. Blessed is lassitude and idleness, behind which no train of consequences drags. Isn't that right, isn't that so, my dears?

"Yet can you be a devotee of such peace, one in which a turbulent maelstrom swirls at all hours of the day? My unbalanced steps aspire to quietude, I know this for sure, but they pursue it across lands in the midst of which my journey's goal vanishes. Now I walk through the land of sinful love.

"Sin ought to be great, supposing it plays out in a tender soul. It ought to be a spectacle with choruses like a Greek tragedy. Whereas mine is a strange sort, not measured by the metrics of power; it is merely pleasurable and terrible.

"And you will say again that guilt is a pleasure, while the feeling of sin is already punishment. No, no, little chaste, fresh-faced souls. You, Clarus, speak daily, urbi et orbi, of sin, though you don't know its essence. Neither do you, Zygmunt. By contrast, Postumus knows lewdness, but of sin and pleasure he knows not..."

And it was Postumus who now sprang to his feet and stammered: "... I'm innocent, innocent, I say! Believe me, Art and Ideas have always been a part of me. What you're thinking of is a phase on the path of the Search for Life... *Not guilty!* ..."

Henryk stared at him with glazed eyes penetrating him with the thought: *You're lying...*

"You are the one who dared do vile deeds. You tore Marysia the Distant from the King so as to cast her yourself at your feet, while she herself remained virtuous with a yearning in her maidenly heart. You have introduced desires among the four of us. You proclaimed to the world and cast derision upon the love of Achilles and Patroclus... Troublemaker!"

Postumus squeezed down alongside Henryk and, after a moment's consideration, watching Henryk's lips twitching with anger, he seethed through gritted teeth, "Judge not others, ac-teur tra-gique."

And he left.

Henryk turned to the priest.

"We've been talking about guilt and punishment. All of you will see penance soon enough. He'll come back. Because inside him is a heart, it's just his soul has rotted..."

AN EVENING TOGETHER

I.

The door creaked softly.

Henryk's room. In the half-light pictures and portraits hung on walls with dark stains. A Madonna of the Flowers. His father's face. Some maiden with nasturtium in her hair. Beneath Dürer's *Melencolia*, a portrait of Henryk. He stubbornly stares at a dagger. Thoughts of death. But when the door creaked the dim lamp's flame flickered, and from the corner Henryk's eyes flashed.

"Is that you?"

"It's me."

He stood beside the lamp so that his long, thick eyelashes could be seen. His pale forehead turns white in the half-light, his eyes glisten. He brings love and his entire self as an offering…

He has come at Henryk's behest. It is the first time he is face to face with bliss. His Hellenic form distinctly stands out against the backdrop of the darkness. Thin silk fabric covers his torso. His legs are bare except for a thick purple cashmere belt that girded his hips. On the belt, embroidery: the Three Marys at the Tomb.

"Master, why are you sad?"

"I think…"

"Banish the thought, I *am* love…"

"And I, pain and terror…"

He sat down next to Henryk. Silence. Henryk's hands seek out his delicate hands. As they sit next to each other in this way a powerful current courses through their joined hands, which are the most perfect instruments of pleasure. A wildness flares up in the eyes of Henryk, who sees in the other boy's pupils the outline of his own face burning with fever.

And suddenly a blaze flared up in their trembling hands!

An impassioned whisper is heard: "I want you… I want you…"

Kissing at a preposterous angle. Torrid and in a daze. After, the head of a sumptuous statue collapsed onto Henryk's lap, and with his mouth he feasts on the pale, parted lips of Diadumenos.

The silence rings with the throb of raging blood and the echo of ecstasy. A fever in his temples. A heaviness and ache in his eyes. The lamp burns out.

Very well, let there be darkness.

His small boyish heart is beating, his lips burn with a craving for kisses, how he swoons and weakly staggers, falls to his knees. How passionate this young soul is, how very strange is this love: meeting, parting ways, crossing paths, anger and bliss—April weather.

Henryk leaves.

The door creaked, then the gate clanged shut—he's gone out into the orchard.

There is no moon, only darkness and the shadows of trees, imaginary phantoms… T E R R O R …

2.

Henryk is speaking: A man can do so very little and all too much…

On a night like this he cannot overcome himself, cannot fill up his depths with sand. Even if there be filth, even if there be miry sin…

And he could annihilate a thousand beings like himself: with fire, with a bloody fist, with iron.

We are here, but far to the east…

Without end the winds whip across this plateau so you can't hear the advance.

But when I look out at the dark horizons, I know thence the tempest comes. Along the roads heavy artillery will rumble and the hooves of the horde will thunder.

Savages may come from the east and in the still of night set the heavens aflame. Our towns will lie in ruins on unhappy lakes, from our villages only cinders will remain.

And blood!... so much blood...

A man can do that... Too much! too much!

And a man can do so little...

He won't fend off the madness that with hurried steps draws nearer.

He won't overcome his fear of the Unknown...

> He stopped, breaking off midsentence.
> The dreadful silence of anticipation.
> A shout ripped through the air:
> "A c t e u r   t r a g i q u e !!!! Ha! Ha!"

Who is shouting?

Rage in his heart: *Who dare call my anguish an act?!!*

His predatory heart is seething, it thirsts for blood. And suddenly Henryk sees that in his abandon lurks madness... and he wants to explode. Dread in his heart... dread, a chill... How very pale is that which crystallizes thought, having passed through the depths of the soul! And how strong those feelings themselves are!

A furtive thought flickers in the soul, lying in wait for itself—counting the days. It flits past and comes back again.

It burrows under the skin, festers, and sprouts up. The thought whispers: *What's it all for? Do you know what all this is for?* A fear of madness... The horror of the human soul... Consciousness of sinful love... The tragic nature of your lack of faith... So many maggots are gnawing at your soul! Stop it... Stop it! Enough!

He's already shouting seductively and fawning like a chimera with tigers' paws.

3.

The door creaked.

Henryk's room, dark, empty, and sort of eerie. He put his ear to the door, behind which unfurls pani Hanka's rainbow of dreams.

A feeble shout: "The End of the FAIRY TALE!..."

And a *bang* in the chamber's four walls!!!

Shouts... murmurs... footsteps... Someone says: "So young." ... Another voice: "He's playing around."

Lights in the corridor. A hubbub.

They're bringing a lamp.

Smoke wafts in the air. A whiff of gunpowder.

Pani Hanka floats toward him like a white apparition. She sits on his bed and asks: "Where's the blood? Does it hurt?..."

With a nimble feminine motion she hides the revolver in the folds of her skirt and strokes Henryk's aching head.

She plays with his hair: "...What were you trying to do, Little Henryk? Little Henryk?...So much to live for, so much to trouble yourself with, you don't have to bear it alone. Promise that you won't do that again... Little Henryk..."

While he rambles in a fever: "My hand twitched. I didn't have the strength to try again... Damned nerves!..."

Then tears flow down his pale cheeks and fall on the pillow. His pursed lips mutter spitefully: "Coward!... coward!...coward!..."

Then the abyss of fever and oblivion, an entire theater of phantoms and dreams.

The last reflexes of a proud will: "... Get out...stop tormenting me... I don't want your pity!..."

And once more a grappling with death. Phantoms. Specters. Ravings.

THEATER IN THE SOUL
Scene One

Henryk is the king.

He's just now stood in Wawel Cathedral on the day of his coronation. His eyes are lowered. At his feet, so many carpets upon which the feet of bishops and princes in ele-gant, tight-fitting shoes stand. The king's brother, Henryk of Głogów, has wonderfully engraved silver spurs on his heels.

Shimmers... glisters of satin... piercing streaks of diamond sparkles... the archbishop's crozier is aflame like an archangelic sword. Everything in a blur of sunlight.

Henryk mechanically repeats the words of the oath. He feels how on his shoulder blade and upper back the greasy fingers of Christ's dignitary anoint him.

And at the same time within him trepidation: God's anointed?... monarch?...

At last the heaviness of the jewels weigh on his head: it's the crown.

Not waiting for the end of the ceremony, he gets up from his knees, walks toward the cathedral doors, wide open to the sun. He treads heavily. Thousands of footfalls behind him.

The entire procession of lords and counts palatine, a gilded retinue in velvets, satins, and silks.

Before him twelve pages in two rows trimmed with azure silk. And one, the thirteenth, in purple.

"Leave me, all of you!"

The king in his castle.

Dusk falls. The enormous windows are already filled with evening's grayness. From them you can see the roofs of the cathedral and the silhouettes of divers spires.

The marble floor shimmers like water... Some kind of shadow on it.

The king claps his hands.

A rustle at the door. The purple page appears, face-to-face with Henryk.

God! That face! Deep hazel eyes—two worlds! Light brown hair cropped above the brow... Who was it I knew? ... Where do I know those eyes from?...

"Diadumenos!!!"

The king rushes toward him, gets tangled up in his coronation mantle, falls...

When he wakens from his faint, he is lying on an ermine in an empty chamber...

Darkness... some faces...

And on the marble lies a crown,

a crown of g o l d - c o l o r e d   p a p e r.

A moan...

Awakening...

Interlude: Reality

Jadwiga, his sad, loving sister bends over Henryk. He lifts his exhausted head... beside her, the priest's stern, swarthy face. They had sat all night beside his bed, thinking about his entire life... Behold, the mighty nobleman laid low— the rot of his trunk for your viewing pleasure. Neither he nor she knows what hangs in the balance in this lonesome soul. They sit at his bedside all night and all the gloomy, rainy morning.

"...My crown, page, my crown..."

Clarus wrings his hands: "What is it, what are you saying, master?..."

And before him appears a vision of a meadow near Lublin and of those bright eyes that now turn red with fever.

In a fever Henryk rolls over toward the wall. He doesn't say a word. The sulking sparrows on the branches glumly chirp. It's raining. Henryk once more sinks into a dream, this time a long, drawn-out, restless one...

Scene Two

He dreams of madness.

Clamor... commotion... hustle and bustle...

Shouts, an uproar, that cause the narrow alleyway to quake. In pursuit! With the remaining strength in his winded body he propels himself forward. The crowd after him. Rocks and curses whizz by, and the rabble's frenzied laughter rends the air.

"C'mon!!! Sic 'im!! Grr! Get him!"

And he runs and falls on the cobblestone.

After—a moment of bewilderment. Bedlam above him, then it subsides, moves away... dies down. A thousand feet had flown past him in a flurry. They hadn't seen... —a triumph!

But that cursed silence after that uproar of the crowd. You can hear how his heart clangs... The blood throbs in the strained veins of his brain, the ebb and flow of this ocean are pounding at his fingertips.

His heart refuses to calm down...

. . . .

"Do you not dance, sir?"

"Unfortunately..."

"Let's take a walk through the garden then."

"I'm at your service, ma'am."

They walk down quiet paths lined with moving trees. The chestnut trees on either side of the path rush past him like the view from the windows of a train carriage. Henryk grows alarmed but keeps the conversation going:

"Do you like music?"

"The Passions, especially Bach's, Palestrina, Handel's."

Beautiful Helen pouts her little lips contemptuously. "And for me, it's Scriabin and Szymanowski."

"In other words, you very much like the latest shipments straight from some Parisian factory for artistic advertising."

"Oh, you!"

Sulking, she walks beside him, beautiful, fragrant, but his heart is flooded by a surge of anxiety. Because the trees are rushing past him, and there, behind his back, they amass into a menacing horde... He turned around.

A shout! Once again an uproar in a cramped alleyway. He rushes, rushes hand in hand with a beautiful doll whose profile is formed not by God but by Żmurko.

They run to the square in front of some Gothic cathedral.

And suddenly their legs, rather than bolting like lightning, get tangled up in a dance rhythm. Laah-la-la, laah-la-la...

They dance in the square. A crowd has formed a large, wide ring encircling them and watches. Their feet float above a little circus rug. He plays a faun's polyphonic pan flute, she whistles with purple lips.

"Stop it!"

"*You* stop!"

"Stop playing!"

"Don't whistle!"

"You said you don't dance!"

"Because I don't dance..."

Sulking again. She has taken off her cap and is walking around the crowd. Her head of dark hair flashes here and there beneath the cloudy sky. Coins, lots of coins... She walks toward him and scatters the coins at his feet. The gold jingles...

"The crown is rolling away!"

A paper crown with glass jewels rolls through the crowd, parting it. He runs after it, after lost majesty.

A strong wind lifts it above the cathedral's towers. He flies up into the air... A game of hide-and-seek. The golden paper will now settle on some gargoyle's stone head, then on the huge fountains' dragon, now it will rest on the balcony's balustrade or inside the rose window above the entrance. Both swirl in the wind's wild rollick. The king and the crown… The crowd roars with glee. Fly! Fly!———horror!!! Falling!!

. . . .

"Pani Jadwiga, the compress on his forehead needs changing already."

"Pan Jan, fetch a little milk from the kitchen, won't you?"

Footsteps, a rustling. *Why is it dark?… Ah, it's evening… Clarus and Jadwiga.*

. . . .

The palace is burning? Let it burn.

The hall's windowpanes flooded with red light. The scorched windows rattle. A river of fire surges inside… *What's this? The underworld?* The currents of the Acheron and the Cocytus, and there, in the darkness of Gothic vaults, the Lethe, the river of oblivion, of peace and quiet.

Is this the underworld or a steelworks?… Maybe it's lava from the heated iron?…

"Fire!!"

"Get out!!!"

But there's no way out of the palace. He runs in vain through the halls, an endless series of chambers. There's no way out! Muffled music: the One-Step. Dreamy, perverse, uncanny sounds... Once more the whirl of a dance. The king dances in the midst of a fire of blazing tongues and of the One-Step's golden-crested wave.

"...Henryk! Henryk!"

Instead of the sun a Kabbalistic sign shines in the sky. In front of Henryk the sage Duskdawn lectures on the Bhagavad Gita.

"Verse 45 of the Samkhya Yoga begins with the words: 'There are three guṇas in the Vedas... The names of these guṇas are sattva, rajas, tamas..' A person in turmoil, like you, is tamas, which means he needs to believe in ghosts, demons, and other bhūtas; you fear them and they torment you... you are in their power."

Henryk turns away from the sage and says contemptuously, "What nonsense."

. . . .

"He's raving, utterly senseless."

"Fever?"

"103."

"It's bad, very bad... But don't worry yourself, pani Jadwiga. Despite that, your brother is going to live, really..."

The doctor shakes his gray head strangely.

. . . .

A meadow, the sun, so many flowers.

What's that? Why this strange body, what kind of creatures are these all around me?

Ah, they're centaurs. And I, too, am the owner of four hooves and a marvelous tail. But if you're half horse, what do you eat: what people eat or grass?

The sun is setting.

The herd of centaurs runs into the woods for the night.

Henryk is with them. All of a sudden he rebels. *Why am I among these horses?*

He turns back toward town.

When you're traveling from Kalinowszczyzna, the silhouettes of the Dominican walls and cathedral are marvelously sketched in the sky. Turrets, belfries, apses, the Trinitarian Tower with such fine, delicate embroidery projected onto the background of the graying sky. But so much red at the base!

The town is empty and quiet. The gas streetlamps are already burning and dusk has flooded the sidewalks. The shops' display windows glow.

The centaur's hooves trudge beneath the low arch of the Krakow Gate. A wide plaza... Three steel fortresses, three tanks. Salvos on the outskirts of town. The centaur stands still, listens... The wind waves a red banner atop town hall... The revolution!!

"Allons enfants de la Patrie" ...

The centaur lifted one hoof, still silent, straining to hear.

Until the triumph of the people's will, the drums banged, crackled. The Lublin Lajkonik rushed down Krakowskie Przedmieście at full gallop...

The shod hooves strike the pavement, falling vigorously like hail. His elegant, silky tail blows about. The centaur flashes by like a July storm and flies far away outside the city to proclaim freedom to the fields.

A meadow, the sun, wildflowers, a river.

He lies on the grass and gazes into the stream. Because something there is shimmering in the depths, something much too luminous and with a sparkle. The glass ruby of the sun blushes scarlet and promises the honey of royal favors. Surrounded by the deposited river ooze, bobbing in rhythm to the drowsy murmur of the waves, a crown flashes from the bottom of the depths, Henryk's crown of paper... Tears, tears, tears...

. . . .

"O Little Henryk, why are you crying?... You can't, baby, you can't..."

"Master..." *What torment this must be...*

Henryk opens his eyes: *Yes, it's them. Clarus and Jadwiga.*

"Am I crying?...it's true... my face is wet... it's nothing, it's just that I... I'm not in pain, only my soul... But I'm happy. I can even sing: *La, la, lala, la, la.*

"Do you know this, Little Jadwiga? It's Bach's Gavotte in D minor... I am dreaming of a forest..."

In the oceanic rustle of trees, a house drowned in dark.

O'er, as though in a Gothic cathedral, hangs a starry arc.

The late evening wave carries a mournful tune,

Amidst the hush of a lulled fairytale forest is heard a pan
        flute's rueful croon…

So bewitchingly it plays to the trees, sky, and star-filled lake,
        they all start to swoon.

From the receding tree line to the moon, some echoes take
        flight from the deepest deep,

And with skirts hiked high above their knees, the maidens
        fair submit to the twirl and leap.

The moon is shining, the pipes are calling, a light but
        lavish shower is falling…

Drowned in the dance of the moonlit night the girlish
        crowd even now is past recalling.

Someone just outside shelters a lit candlestick with an
        irradiated hand:

Balladyna ventures out to Grabiec on a hot, sultry May
        night just as planned…

All the windows are dark but the house does not sleep. You
        can make out murmurs, noiseless kissies.

Now all lads are like demigods—like sylvan nymphs, all
        missies.

So high in the tree's branches, his eyes melting into the
        moon's face, or so it seems,

Sits small Diadumenos all by himself while about his own
strange life he dreams…

Interlude: Reality and Dream

"Pani Hanka, why is he constantly dreaming about
some boy?"

"You don't know?"

Here Hanka leans toward the doctor's ear and whispers something with a half smile. "Woman!" The doctor
likewise relays the matter in a hushed voice to the three
young Dulski girls who very much adore Henryk's poetic
talent and had come to ask about his health.

His sister knows and Clarus knows, but they keep quiet.

And there it is—laughter. The fat belly of the jovial
old codger bounces with laughter. Pani Hanka's splendid
mouth winces ironically.

And suddenly an outburst! Their horrified souls per-
ched on the edge of their seats, cowering… Not sticking to
the performance, in the middle of the interlude, Henryk
breaks character and shouts, "Curtain! I'm acting!!"

. . . .

Rome. The Papal Altar in St. Peter's Basilica.

The tatters of the royal mantle on Henryk's shoulders,
dirty, disheveled ermines, and a paper crown atop his tou-
sled hair…

The crowd already knows about my love affair…

What on earth should I call what's on so many snickering, gleefully-amused mouths—that there is such a fool who does not love women? Stupid indeed; after all, the breeding instinct can only be satisfied with "love" for a woman.

O foolish little man, whatever anxiety about women you have you carried with you from your family home!

O little fellow, what you believed in were the sketches of Rops and Beardsley!

You were in love once and nobody knew the depth of your love. Nobody was troubled by your anguish—only one friend, Zygmunt…

You fell in love all over again with a woman, a young girl, fresh and sweet smelling like a boy. This time nobody knew about it, except your sister…

Now you've fallen in love with a boy, a few people know and they laugh to their hearts' content.

It is I, o my most beloved cattle, the one committing the sin of stupidity!

A voice in the crowd: "Acteur tragique!"

Yet Henryk, beside himself with grief, did not feel the blow. His thoughts whisper: "Take your revenge, strike a blow into the heart of the riff-raff!"

And suddenly the corners of Henryk's mouth pucker with boundless contempt, and his face becomes demonically repulsive with the threat of vengeance. He mutters spitefully: "That's quite enough for today's sermon."

. . . .

The priest bent down over Henryk's possessed eyes and cries out: "Master, wake up... I'm afraid... what has gotten into your soul?"

Jadwiga is crying in the corner, but maybe she's not crying, maybe she's just covered up her eyes before this horror. Her heart cries out with fear, "Brother.."

It's raining, the branches outside the window are swaying, a birch creaks in the strong wind.

Truth. This is reality... Life...

How these dreams wear me out...

Scene Three

| Maestoso: | His last words the Lord said From His shoulders hung His head... |

Henryk hears the moan of a thousand bosoms, of a thousand souls that believe.

Just what kind of faith is this that endures ages without fading? There's not a single bitter note in his soul. He sits in the tower and listens to the Good Friday Passion.

It's dark. The vaulted windows are full of stars. The church's vast shell is filled with singing. The bells absorb the human moan into their own monstrous cavities and softly grumble.

An overwhelming seriousness in Henryk.

His thoughts flit past: ...*Why can't I believe? I alone, with my own impetus, cast myself outside the circle of faith, and now I long for... the Church?... No, I can't come back here...*

And this faith that unknowingly grows in my soul is much too simple, my critical judgment doesn't want to accept it. So so many months of my life have been in search of something else. I always tried to look beyond the mirrors that chance had set up all around me. I was searching for something, and my longing kept saying that there would be something higher... but all I found was a theory. O bitterness!

A shadow on the tower steps.

It creeps in the dark over the scaffolding, higher, higher ... until it reaches Henryk.

It sat down opposite on the crossbeam of an enormous bell.

It's Postumus. His words flow with a hoarse, wise whisper: "I! I! I'm here already, tragédien, and I'll tell you what was and what will be. Do you want to hear it? But even if you didn't want to listen, I am going to tell you. Because I believe in fate, in Fate with a capital F. I have discovered the unshakeable mathematical formulas of psychology. I'm like a wizard. After your deeds, I know what's going to happen to you.."

"I'm not even curious."

"My mathematical calculations say that you have

abandoned your faith even as you continue searching for it. Instead, of course, you found a theory and you are putting it into practice. You'll meet with disaster here. You say that you alone are intentionally creating guilt and punishment. But do you know what your punishment is? And do you know that your greatest sin is hidden from your consciousness? And do you know that what you consider a sin, this love for a boy, is childish nonsense?

"And if you get so tired of this, how will it be with actual guilt, how great will your punishment be? Do you know? *You* are creating it?! Maggot! Vermin!"

"Get away from me, tempter. Leave my miserable sight!"

"Are you angry, master? Strut and swagger and do great things so long as the strong wind of anguish doesn't snap you in two. Your well-reasoned faith will crush you. But don't forget to put that theory of yours into practice, or else I'll think that my predictions spooked you."

Anger swells up in Henryk's dark eyes. Instead of sorrowful songs of bitter regrets, he hears only his own roiling, throbbing blood.

"Silence! Do not sneer! You do not exist! You are a phantom of my wicked, foul thoughts. You resist, but I am your lord. You nip, but you will fall at my feet, beast."

A blaze in Henryk's hair, a storm over his furrowed forehead. Postumus fell onto a bell as if apologetic and disheartened. He grovels. He slithers away from bell to bell toward the stairs. Until, in front of the last one, he will seize it and roar into the bell that thundered with an excruciating echo...

"Boom!!! Booom!!!" the bell blares. "OOooOm!!! OOooO!"

The Sigismund Bell rings out... The other bells grow alarmed.

Everything in Henryk cracked. Both his strained nerves and his blazing white-hot anger. Falling downward... The abyss... Awakening.

Interlude: Reality

Music. The mixed, faint scent of flowers. Heliotropes and asters, it seems. A minuet by Mozart, the one with the enchanted flute that makes the intertwined couples dance. A streak of light, fragrance, and melody flow through the door into the dark room.

A shadow in the bright rectangle of the door.

"Is that you, Little Jadwiga?"

"It's me. You're not asleep? Perhaps you're not well?"

"No, no, it's just how the fever burns."

"Eat some oranges... you'll quench your thirst."

The tropical scent of golden fruit. The trace of sunny Italian orchards. A fleeting thought about the hands of the *Mona Lisa*. So even with a fever he still remembers her?

"Little Jadwiga, you're so pretty in this darkness, with tuberose in your black hair. Your luxurious Rubenesque dress accentuates your womanliness. And all night you have been whirling about in the atmosphere of the ball, of the music... There was a ball, wasn't there?"

"Yes, Little Henryk, go to sleep already, sleep, little brother, and stop with the compliments... Good night."

She went out.

A new shadow in the doorway. Very small, approaching without a murmur. It is Diadumenos. When he looks back, his thin eyebrows and mysterious eyes can be seen in the golden light. Without a breath, he flows lithely on bare feet like an apparition.

He's beside Henryk. He leans over him and whispers, "Master.."

There is no response, but in the darkness a restless, feverish breathing can be heard, and the heat radiates from the patient. A delicate hand slides beneath the pillow and pulls out from there a parcel, a bundle of letters. Maryla's letters.

Light footsteps float to the fireplace where a red flame crawls over the dying coals. In this light Diadumenos thumbs through the letters and tosses them one by one into the fire... Her words go up in smoke...

I don't want anything from you anymore... This sadness clouds my heart...

...come for Wigilia, white, white with snow, on the same street as usual. I'll be waiting, good and loving...

...spring will come for you and for me, just don't be sad for me...

Her words go up in smoke.

His little wild heart hates its rivals. It wants to have all his heart and all his love. He bends down over Henryk, kisses his burning lips and disappears.

Scene Four

I.

A winged prayer resides in the king's heart. He looks at the Franciscan stained-glass windows and admires them. Rainbows of luminous colors materialize into shapes, lines, and flowers. Thorn bushes had sprung up over their holy heads. Instead of fragrance, heavenly jubilation inhabits the flowers. Heavenly jubilation instead of fragrance. His eyes are so shaded, so illumined by the light of the colors, that they cannot see the dark walls or the soaring ceiling.

Stained-glass windows as though suspended in dark nothingness—celestial apparitions. Especially strange is the one with Saint Francis, Christ's poor wretch. His pale palms glow—palms on which ruby stigmata ooze blood...

The king dreams, losing himself in his fascination. He isn't dreaming about anything else but Saint Francis's little flowers, about his love and his beautiful deeds that flower so colorfully on the stained glass.

Happiness inhabits a faith of loving and forgiving.

The saint descends on a beam of sunny luminance from that stained-glass window. And he lifts the king up from his knees and leads him along. They crossed the length of the empty church, toward the organ they go. In the choir the saint points to a bench and tells him, "Sit down, if Thou art not a man."

The king did not sit but looks at the saint with astonished eyes.

"Look up."

The king's otherwise calm soul is bursting apart with hurricanes of rapture; it is intoxicated with eternity. Above him, God the Father Himself in the splendor of power.

"Peel off the riches of Thy garments," says the saint. "Fall to the dust before Thy Creator and think not. Let Thy soul be humbled in the dust lest a rebellious thought creep forth from Thy brain."

The king, obedient to the words of the wellspring of faith and love, casts off his velvets and white silk. He is left naked in the choir; only on the wrist of his left hand a gold chain jingles and glistens.

The wretch of the Lord Jesus did utter, "Into the dust! Humble Thyself, if Thou be a man!"

"And you?"

"I am going to the orchard, to the golden honeybees and the azure sky," smiled the luminous shadow.

Amazement again in the royal eyes. But Francis explains the matter; with a gentle gesture of his pale hands he marks off the difference: "Thou, a man, must pray. But I am holy."

And he left him on his own.

2.

"Welcome, Julian!"

Julian rises from the stool and squeezes his brother's hand.

"Tell me, when did you get back? How on earth did you live in captivity?"

The king sat down on a Bronowice chest, painted in various colors, and listens. On him, black boyish clothes with white lace — Hamlet's outfit. Behind sheer curtains of tulle that cover the open window a quiet dusk descends.

Julian recounts his story to him: how despair and hope took hold of him, how a serious illness struck him down, how much abject misery there was in that distant eastern land.

He tells a tale about Moscow's golden capital. How like a dream the holy Kremlin looks, like a dream...

When it's already dark and cozy in the room, the brothers become real Brothers, and a pure gold thread of feelings and understanding already binds them.

The king complains, "I'm looking for a meaningful, important life; I don't know where to find it. I locked away my pain on a few sheets of paper in order to rid myself of it. I thought that if I were to express my sorrows it would be easier for me, but no... not easier."

Julian stares sternly at his brother's fever-changed face. "Be strong and brave! Everything advances toward death and eternity (possibly nothingness). It will come despite all our struggles. So if it is going to come, it's better to meet it with a brave heart than with a bitter smirk.

"Be strong!"

"And my yearnings?"

"I know it's difficult to cast them aside, so difficult... Sometimes it comes unexpectedly, the nostalgia of cool, hazy moonlit nights in a deserted city with a gas streetlamp's flicker and faint glimmer. It's easy to be downhearted then."

"Yes, Julian, I know, there are such moments... after which the grinder is cranked again: vapid grins, life... if this is life... But it's late already and time for supper. Will you come along to the table?"

"I don't like the ruckus of your banquet hall."

"Then farewell, Brother!"

3.

With a gentle graze, the king's broad, sultry lips touch the somber eyes of Marysia the Distant.

"Why are you so quiet?"

"I'm sad. Whenever we're alone and so close my heart is troubled and tormented. You seem to me like my fate, you are so unclear and unfathomable."

"You see, dear: as for me, I am growing tired of these feelings by which you live. This love of ours from under an evil star... maybe it's Arcturus."

He made a slow gesture, his hand pointing to a spot in the distant night sky. And it became even sadder for both of them.

"Marysia," he began again, "wouldn't it be better for us to go our separate ways?"

"Don't say that!"

"But think: when you arrive cheerful, there is bitterness inside me; when I'm up to my ears in merriment, you're bitter and sad. Why is that? Let us part ways. There will be no more of this sadness."

Marysia cries. Her voice trembles.

Glances... glances... A sigh... An inaudible whisper...

"Don't throw it all away. Come back. You'll see, our next meeting will be cheerful and lovely, like the first leaves, like the chrysanthemums in your garden."

But the king sadly thinks: *I can't give up. You have to come again and wear yourself out. Ah, fate!*

"I'm leaving, Marysia. The guards are lowering the bridges."

"But you will come back, won't you? Won't you?" —her voice, swollen with tears, pleads.

Glances, tears, a whisper...

A sigh...

4.

Marysia sat down at the loom. She keeps dropping everything. She grumbles to herself, she complains to the walls of her father's cottage...

Why did he meet me? Why did he take hold of my heart...

Who is placing these chasms between us? And she wistfully sings:

> *Hey, sing to me, sing, little Highlander brother,*
> *Hey, so that my heart won't break from grief!*
> *Hey, give us, Mary, a little sunshine and good weather,*
> *Hey, so that my young prince might see!*
> *He's like an eagle high atop his eagle perch,*
> *And I—a wounded doe who for death awaits!*
> *Hey, we fell in love though there's still much more to learn,*
> *And now it's our hearts that grief and sadness embrace!*

She is singing and weaving golden chrysanthemums on linen. And for the torrential downpour of her tears she doesn't see that it has gotten brighter in the cottage. Saint Francis stood beside her and says, "If lilies could speak, they would have the very same voice. What are you singing about, girl?"

"I'm singing my sadness."

"What kind of sadness is it?"

"My most beloved's heart is harsh and fierce like a wild beast's."

"I tamed the wolf of Gubbio and I can tame him too. Where does he live?"

"In the castle, my good man."

"Aha, it seems you aim higher than the girls from these parts. Surely it's the king, the unfortunate Henryk."

Marysia said nothing, looking out the window at the field. In the stubble, beneath the white sky a whole pack of dogs, like sheep. Trumpets drone, hunters rush in pursuit toward the Tatras.

The hunt.

"If you here really are holy and want to redress my lot, go to him! He is here, on a black horse."

"But I already know him. He was the one who marveled at me at the Franciscan Church in Krakow. It was he who lay in the dust before pan Wyspiański's stained-glass images! He is difficult, but I will go."

Marysia's thoughts as he bounded toward the door: *If you really were to get him to return to me, even if only for one evening, I would indeed be completely yours, my saint!*

A shadow on the cottage. Marysia looks up. A bandit had entered. His hair in braids, a belt three spans wide, trousers beautifully embroidered in red.

"Girl, I will return him to you for one evening. Then you will be mine."

"How?"

"That's my business. He will be yours."

"Are you not lying? Swear! On your pistol."

The bandit places his hand on the butt of the pistol and swears: "On my bandit honor, on the Wiśnicz gallows, on my soul and this pistol."

The king enters the cottage. He stood in the doorway. He recognized the bandit.

"Heel, cur. Stay put, Postumus!"

I.

Outside the walls, on a dark, overcast night, at the foot of some duke's buildings is a lane, fragrant and quiet with gardens like the walls along the Vistula. There—the two of them.

Marysia: "Why do your eyes glow with this incredible brightness?"

The king: "Because you are beautiful and sweet-smelling. The tangle of your tresses smells like Goplana's fleece, tied by swallows."

Marysia: "You love my hair?"

The king: "The whole of you . . . only I don't know you."

Marysia: "It is the same with you."

King: "You know, I will give you a name: Marysia the Unknown or the Distant."

Marysia: "Very well, my lord. I love you, so I submit to all you require."

King: "O slave."

Marysia: "O sorrow!... Yes, I am your slave."

King: "Thou art woman, the light of the world. From such as you are born Manu, Zarathustra, and Christ."

Marysia: "Why do you not believe me? Are you trying out my heart?"

King: "As I want to know who will always be with me from here on out."

Marysia: "O Christ!"

King: "Woman, give me your lips. This kiss will be the first and the last. I am going in search of the Grail, or perhaps the abyss."

Marysia: "My lips? Here they are."

He leaned her back, trembling, like the strings on a violin. He tilted her until the castle's dark mass reflected in her pupils, until her dark chestnut mane brushed the dust on the cobblestone.

Silence.

Postumus suddenly emerges. Up until now he had been the king's shadow. He stood behind them grimacing, and he blesses their strange kiss.

2.

Someone had stopped beneath the trees. The fireplace's red glow cast a fantastic light on the figure of the king and blinded him. The king sees the apparition—he cannot see who it is. The apparition moves toward him. Bowing to the ground.

"Is that you?... I. Are you alone, king?"

"I am."

"Can we talk?"

He leaned against the hearth and whispers with regret, "King, you're playing a part in a comedy. Why are you tormenting her?"

"I can't help it. I've already parted ways with her three times. Yet my longing draws me toward her. A lofty, sacred longing..."

"But you wound her every time you see her."

"Because she desires my lips, their quiet bliss. While I desire only her sad eyes. I love her as a marvelous statue, and she loves me as a man."

"I once loved her. I stopped."

The king silently looks at Zygmunt. His eyes darken.

Silence.

"Hallelujah, my lilies are blooming!"

The Poor Man of Christ enters the chamber singing. Having looked at them, he smiles, opens the windows wide. "Let some light in here."

And evening scents from the gardens and orchards waft in. The shadow of the cathedral looms in the starry sky.

He leaned out the window, gripping a rosary in his palm.

"...Look, Adam, you brooding philosopher. Is Eve tempting you here every day? What a wonderful garden!

So many roses! It is worth being merely a witness to love..."

"Or to sin," the king gloomily retorts.

"No, this paradise merits love and affection. Or else what would these roses and flowers be for? What would the divine beauty of these lawns' greenery be for? And these trees laden with fruit—for what? This is the world —our mother—love."

"But it was man who invented sin..."

"A strong person will shrug it off or trample it beneath his feet," Zygmunt said with faith.

The saint contemplated the enormous sun. "For what reason could there be so much light—? Is it for tracking down our sin? Surely—it shines for love... The world! The world! beloved thorny roses! Precious weeds and thistles! Glowworms, butterflies, and birds! I'm coming to you! Remain in health, good people!"

And he nimbly, soundlessly heads out into the orchard. His robe fluttered—and he was gone.

They look at each other.

"This is difficult for me," Zygmunt grumbles.

The king is silent. After all, Marysia does say his heart is hard.

"Oh so difficult."

The man cries; he does not cover his face; great pitiful tears flow. Royal pride whispers, "What sentimentality!"

But his soul also feels tears inside itself, maybe even heavier ones...

"Henryk, kiss me, like a brother."

A brotherly kiss—they will be friends forever.

Francis's voice rings out in the orchard:

> *My green frogs croak!*
> *O the dew they drink*
> *From lily goblets sealed with cork*
> *When the sun begins to sink!*

3.

Warm orange tones. A sweltering heat. Greenery sprinkled with sand and sun-drenched gold dust. Some garden or happy isles since surrounded by white-capped water like a mane.

Strange shapes—slender like poplar trees. Billowing flame-colored bushes burgeon at their feet. Tawny grass. Muted melodies and songs drift through the garden.

"Magdalene, you will follow Christ and abandon your former loves; the marvelous eyes of your princes, nights filled with folly, possession."

Jędrek Cajka, a nimble, lithe boy leads Marysia through these marvelous lands. All of a sudden, the luminescence of daybreak on the road and standing before them a six-winged Seraph. It raises its hands marked with stigmata and sweetly says, "Marysia, come Thou unto my wings… Walk Thou singing with me through mountains and forests.

Cherish Thou only lilies and fowl… Black Lake and Eye of the Sea… Only the whole world and nothing more. For Thou knowest not how to cherish people."

But she, sad, says, "Hence away, begone, Saint Francis. You two have already deceived me once. I am now amusing myself with the boy. Let the king know."

"I haven't deceived you at all—it's just I could not break his hard heart. He has humbled himself before God—I have seen it. To do so before a woman, that he refuses."

"What will become of us?"

They stand there, not speaking. Some sweet scent reaches them, some kind of purple birds cut across the azure sky. Hefty oranges fall at the foot of the trees onto the rust-colored lawn.

Until Jędrek bellows, "You've blocked our path!"

Having looked into Cajka's eyes, the saint departed.

They continue their walk through the delightful garden.

Three people—two Highlanders and an old woman—are picking figs from a tree.

One stands on a ladder and plucks figs, tossing them into the woman's lap. While the third, with a shepherd's axe, keeps an eye out for the Hesperidean maidens since this orchard was theirs. They are stealing.

Jędrek laughs and leans toward Marysia, "Marysia, I would jump into the fire for you, and I would carry you in my arms like a tiny infant… Are you happy with me?"

"I am happy, so happy. Why is it so deserted here?"

"Would you rather have them watching us?"

"No. It's just so unnerving."

"Are you afraid? With me?"

"You have such strange eyes. They're smoldering."

"Marysia!"

"What do you want?"

"*You! You!*"

They sank down on the garden wall. The golden fields are watching them, watching as Jędrek takes Marysia in his arms, roughly, on the spot. Marysia weeps.

I.

From beneath the fountain's silver spume, flowing unheard into the uplands, trickles a stream into a valley full of flowers. Crocuses, daisies, dandelions—white, red, gold. By the water a little apple tree with tiny heavenly fruit. Little Józio tries to reach the branches, he clambers, full of childlike grace, toward the fruit that his dark eyes desire. —Staszek, an older blue-eyed boy, stood at the bend of the trickling creek. His hands are full of crocuses. He tosses one into the water and follows with his eyes the movement of the enchanted rafts.

The king and Julian watch from the shade of an arcade.

"It's us," they say to each other. "It's us."

The sun has vanished. Clouds.

The wiii… the whiiistling wiiinds…

The trees bent and shook in the clutches of the wind.

Against the backdrop of rain a seaside cliff can be seen.

On the cliff a man in a black overcoat that the storm thrashes like a sail. At the base of the cliff are several figures who in desperation shout out to him, "Master! We love you! Why is your heart indifferent?"

But he stares at the distant mountains on the horizon.

"Go away, people! Leave me alone! I want to climb to new heights where there's sharp icy air, where there's power, where there's health."

Everyone has the right to a Postumus.

That man's Postumus mocks with deliberate pathos. "Go! Through the storm! Through the ocean! Lay down your life!"

"That's you on the cliff," the king says. "It's you, Julian."

The sky cleared. The sun, at its zenith. The earth, fresh and fragrant after the rain. The forests puff smoke like censers.

A Hesperian Garden apparition.

Enchanted shadows wander around. Enchanted as they have encroached upon the land of fantasy, poetry, and semi-happiness.

A boy and a girl walk there and back.

In the middle of a clearing they meet up and part ways all over again in order to once more rendezvous. And so it goes on and on forever.

Whenever they part ways, their yearning, in the form of a shadow, stretches out beyond recognition. When they pass by each other, glancing into each other's eyes, their tiny, shriveled yearning lies down at their feet. It cowers like a dog.

"It's you," Julian says. "You and Marysia, or maybe you and Truth."

2.

Julian brought his face closer to his brother's face and speaks strange words. His steely pupils shine sternly, unrelentingly.

"A strong man must hold a woman in contempt. Do you not feel that everything in you breaks down just because you delude yourself with love? If you love, it's nothing, but if they love you, it's destructive. Then you fester, and you can't find a way out.

"You remember your words: 'I cannot love her and I cannot help but love her.' So get out from under your heart! Or else your strength will wither away."

The king began to shake helplessly, wringing his hands. "How then? How?"

"Leave her!"

"I can't!"

"Put her out of your mind!"

"It's beyond my control!"

"You must or you'll squander all that you are!"

"My longing will always lead me back to her."

"That's exactly it...this condition of the human soul."

Both became lost in thought. The brother, with a trembling voice, eventually says, "Forgive me for introducing a new torment into your soul. I can see for myself that it is beyond your control. Stay here and consider my words!"

He leaves, supported by a blue pageboy. For a long time after, their footsteps could still be heard in the castle's cavernous hallway.

Midnight had passed a long time ago already, as the candles are burning down.

"Page, a Bible!"

A young boy with light flaxen hair and adorned with sky-blue silk appears.

On the prie-dieu he sets out the Holy Scripture and trims the candles' wicks.

With a gesture from the king the chamber is empty.

Postumus Porco emerges from a dark corner as if from beneath the ground and turns the pages of the Bible. Having found the passage, he reads aloud, "...if thy eye offend thee, pluck it out..."

The king sprang to his feet. He paces the room from one corner to another with broad strides. The moon has darkened. A candle has toppled over. It's dark. A mood like in Lady Macbeth's castle.

Postumus catches a whiff of the king's thoughts and mutters, "The smell of blood is not unpleasant."

But the king is struggling with himself.

"Am I really so weak? No, I have strength. I do! Who dare say that there is no power in this chest? I will go through blood, through sin, through everything that night and evil forces place in my path.

"Raise the curtains! The show must go on! Once more, to the stage!!!"

3.

Jędrek Cajka was cutting hay, he was cutting by moonlight because—heaven forbid!—during the day how the heat sweltered. He swings his scythe while looking at Marysia's cottage. It seems to him that there's some kind of ruckus, and shouts can be heard, but he continues cutting. Suddenly a shot flashed! An echo rang out through the mountains. A second bang, a third. A brawl.

Clutching the scythe against his shoulder, he ran like the wind on swift feet. It's empty—the farmyard... an eerie silence.

Old Samek Rohacz was lying on the doorstep with his head terribly smashed. Blood was puddling, and a trickle was oozing from the threshold. By the moonlight it appeared black. Next to Samek a second body, still warm. An unknown man with his arms spread out with a shepherd's axe gruesomely splitting his forehead. Cajka examined him: a Reiter from the royal cavalry.

Fear gripped him.

He looked into the dark cottage and shouted, "Marysia!"

Silence.

He sat down on a rock and wept. What on earth can he do against the king? He cries and cries until it became light. Dawn. He threw his scythe on the ground.

"I am going to the king. I will perish—death at last! I'm not even scared. After all, more than once have I looked into the abyss."

And he set off with great strides toward Krakow.

He's walking and thinking: *I'm not afraid of death, but he is the king. The richest farmer in all of Podhale is nothing compared to him. He is after all the king.*

"You'll go and be killed," says Vengeance.

"I'm not going—he's the king after all," whispers Jędrek.

He took a look at the road and here in a sun-drenched aurora Saint Francis appears and stretches out his hands toward him.

"Turn back… you're not going at all."

"I will go!" Jędrek protested, "it's my concern, not yours."

"And your work?"

Sooth! Jędrek still has a day's work in the quarries to pay off his debt. He's turned back. It's deserted by the rock. All's clear. He took out dynamite charges and a pickax from their hiding place. He dug out a hole, placed the charge, lit the fuse, and dove behind a boulder. Kaboom! The rocks were blasted to bits. Jędrek placed a second charge, lit it, bolted. He is thinking: *today I work, tomorrow I'll go to Krakow… Why didn't it go off…* He went over… it had gone out. He bent down and blew on the fuse. How the thunder roars!!! Jędrek collapsed onto the rocks without his eyes.

A green Swiss pine bends down over him and murmurs: "Thou shalt not oppose the Saint. You're not going anywhere, Skinny, but to your grave…"

4.

The sun bloodily sets like never before. Against the crimson sky grim silhouettes of skeletal, mournful trees. And among the poplars the silhouette of a tall scaffold. An executioner with sword, a block with red splotches glistening in the sun. To the right, the Royal Castle; on the left, the Franciscan Church.

The crowd buzzes and babbles, milling about in anticipation.

The king walked out onto the terrace. In the sunset's crimson blush an ugly and evil face can be seen, with eyes in which the dusk lies hidden, lurking. The gold and silken mantle stretched over him casts a reflection on the face and crown of the king.

Vivid golden, billowing silk.

Surmas blare to the four corners of the world. It is the king's wish that his love should die gloriously as befits a royal mistress. Below, helmets glinted. Reiters escort Marysia to the scaffold. A priest accompanies her. No, not a priest but Saint Francis.

The sun dims as they step onto the reddened platform.

The poor barefoot wretch in a torn habit takes from her lips a final earthly and pardoning kiss.

The kiss was chaste. It transformed into the white dove that Francis had hid in his hand. Then he smiled at the king and floated through the air to the Franciscan window, stepping into the stained glass and freezing into place.

The king removes the crown from his head and places it in the hands of the pageboy. "Put it on her head."

The golden crown glimmered against Marysia's dark hair. Her narrow, expressionless eyes regard the king. At first they are untroubled, loving even. But then blearing.

Whoosh! The blade came down.

Brass surmas blare, drowning out the sound of the rolling head. The crown falls off and flutters in the wind, far away, into the Vistulan water, which the paper crown soaks up before sinking.

The king, leaning over the balustrade of the terrace, stares at these apparitions with wide eyes and clutches his chest: "It hurts!"

The sun has been snuffed out. It's dark but for a blaze of clouds in the sky.

FRIENDS

In charming, quiet Słobódka health returns to Henryk. And since it's spring, he has gathered his friends around him and they all together delight in the leaves just now unfurling on the trees, the tiny, sticky leaves of poplar, birch or oak.

All day long Henryk lies in the sun in the moss of woodland hills and listens to the friendly conversations. There is Zygmunt, Father Clarus, Madonna Maria, and even Achilles and Patroclus. Henryk is listening just now to one such discussion. The participants of this Symposium are pontificating on art.

Now Clarus: "I am but a longing for creativity. Whatever I paint—it's full of belabored thought and likewise lifeless, convoluted symbols. And yet I harbor so many real feelings for great Art and thus would I long to possess it…"

Zygmunt: "You always write it with a capital *A*, but it's precisely too much longing in you, not enough accomplishment in deed, fulfillment."

Clarus: "So create, not longing for, not thinking about art?"

Zygmunt: "Don't create art, only yourself…"

Achilles: "It's like us, Patroclus and me. We create ourselves in our military life and in our love life."

Clarus: "To the point, dears, to the point. Let us talk about art."

Achilles: "Wha—? Do you not consider the art of living the greatest thing of all?"

Madonna: "Or the art of kindness?"

Zygmunt: "Or the art of sacrifice?"

"Or the art of suffering?" whispers Henryk.

Clarus: "Ah, five heads and five opinions. I only wanted to propose that we return to the conversation about art in a less expansive sense."

Madonna Maria: "It's difficult to talk about a given topic. But why is our dear Patroclus sitting silent and daydreaming?"

Patroclus, who had sat down at a distance, turns his head.

"I was thinking about love... That it's good, most wonderful, though bitter..."

Madonna: "How do you know that, kiddo?"

Patroclus: "I didn't learn it from books... I know from my own experience."

Henryk's mouth winces painfully. They noticed. Nobody breaks the silence.

. . . .

On some other day Henryk and Madonna Maria were once more sitting by the lake. She was telling him about her childhood. In her story there were lots of aromas from the Polish village, of the morning crowing of the cocks, and of the nights full of stars. She liked when he listened to her curiously like a child. She only resented his biting irony. She still saw those colors that for him had already faded.

While they were talking in this way in the silence of the evening, she brought up God. "I believe that God watched over my childhood and that God will continue to watch over me."

"Which one?"

She didn't understand so he asked again.

"Which one? Was it Zielna, Divine Mother of the Herbs, or the angel Anielska or Gromniczna, She of the Thunder Candle with Wolves?"

"How can you, Henryk? Are there really so many gods? Are we pagans then?"

"Yes, that's it, Madonna Maria. Instead of believing in Kupala, today we believe in the Feast of St. John the Baptist. Instead of the old Slavic deities Łada, Nyja, and Dzidzileyla, we have She Who Protects Us on the Day of Our Death, Who Commands Us To Sow the Fields and Blesses the Fields... Do be a patriot, walk among the people and spread the truth. Each field should flourish with its own flowers."

"No, you're lying, Henryk! Christ is in the soul of this people!"

"Christ? No, Jesse in the form of the Man of Sorrows is sitting at the intersections of roads across wide, golden Poland. That is our Christ. In Lithuania beneath a rusty little roof you'll meet a wooden Pensive Christ. It's also him—Jesse."

"So you're reverting to paganism?"

"No, I'm only making my way toward a new life. My new life has to be consistent with my faith so that there won't be this torment of discord with which we now live. So that there won't be this sham unity of the world but something genuine. Let us allow the people to believe in a pagan Christ because that connects faith to life. And let us bring about this one faith all throughout the land. Because among us you subsist on something different from me and Clarus, something different from Zygmunt. And the people struggle, powerless. Hence the sects, hence the fairytales about the national church, the Mariavites, Polish Buddhists, Nietzscheans. Hence the Tolstoyans and mystics."

"So to reinvigorate the people you'll well nigh create the nation anew. . ."

"And thereafter to wield it in my hand like a sword—unified, powerful, terrible. . ."

His eyes flashed. Without warning he looked away and uttered softly, "I want to have the greatest and strongest of nations. . ."

"That's what you're thinking about? What then? Henryk!" Her voice was trembling, she didn't know why.

But he himself was already frightened. He somewhat weakly waved his hand and lowered his head to his chest.

For a long time they stared at the lake. Finally he spoke: "Do you happen to know... what... a paper crown... is...?"

. . . .

In the evening when he was sitting by the window with half-closed eyes, a song from far off troubled his dreams.

There were swings creaking and from all corners of Słobódka this Byelorussian song floated in the air, cheerful in content but mournful in its drawn-out, truly autumnal melody:

> *When I was young and oh so sma-a-a-all*
> *My mama rocked me, rocked me a-a-a-all!*
> *And when I grew up tall and stro-o-o-ong,*
> *The boys started to sing a rocking so-o-o-ong!*

He and Zygmunt are dreaming in this musical silence. You can also hear the breath of the lake which has just thawed out and is full of evening blue.

"This is earthly love," uttered Zygmunt.

These words bring to both of their minds a bizarre painting by Titian. Two lifeless figures seated at the basin of a fountain: one in a robe with long, sharp, rather stiff creases. She leans against the edge of the trough, in her other hand she holds a small bunch of flowers. She has eyes full of mystery, and on her shoulders, marvelous golden hair.

By contrast, the second figure is completely adorned in the bounty of nudity. The same face, only the eyes are without that unearthly solemnity. On the other side of the basin a cupid leans over the water. Behind them a small cluster of trees and the vast, sweeping countryside. The grass—vert d'émeraud. The front face of the basin—like blanc de Chine.

Amor Sacro e Amor Profano. Sacred and Profane Love.

Zygmunt continues to weave his thought further, certain that Henryk remembers about Titian.

"Amor Profano is as naked as Mother Earth because motherhood is the goal of earthly love. All women on earth are mothers. They all serve their own god according to their strength, and since an essential soul can be found in woman both far and wide, then the exceptions only prove the rule. Just think of your sister Madonna Maria."

Henryk says, "But heavenly love is the Unknown. Behold a field for the Conqueror: to seize terrae incognitae from the Mystery."

"This is what you dream about?"

"No, my dream reaches for something further."

"And the implementation, the putting into action?" Zygmunt asks feverishly.

"My deeds are in the dreaming,"—Henryk responds with reluctance and a lack of faith. And they remain silent.

TIDINGS

They were eating lunch. The shaded terrace of the porch was filled with the scent of sweet peas and nasturtiums. Fantastically carved leaves of wild grapevine cascaded over the trellis. Everyone had settled at the table on the porch. They were cheerful and strangely silent.

Just as huge, bursting pomegranates were being brought in on a wooden plate, the sound of hooves on the road to Słobódka rang out in front of the porch.

A magnificent rider on a galloping horse of unheard-of beauty. His hair blew about in a golden halo that flashed and faded on his Greek head. His strong hands held firmly the powerful steed.

Like an apparition! Bellerophon on Pegasus!

And in front of the porch the horse rears up, its gray body towering, and whirls around, stopping beneath the oak, so that its monstrous hooves are suspended over the table. The rider at last restrained him. He dismounted. He walks up to Henryk. They shake hands and introduce themselves.

"Włodzimierz!"

"Potocki!" calls Madonna Maria, who had seen him as he stood in aquiline pensiveness in the Wawel Chapel.

With their eyes the rest silently devour the marvelous figure and wonderful head.

He squeezes everyone's hands.

"I am with you," he says. "I am with you."
And on Easter Day it was, on Easter Day.

PRONUNCIATION GUIDE

a	as in *father*
ą	(nasal *a*) *on* as in *hone* but without the tongue closing on the *n*; before *b* and *p* it sounds more like *om* as in *home*
b	as in *boy*
c	*ts* as in *cats*
ch	as in Scottish *loch* or German *ach* (can also be pronounced the same as *h*)
cz	*ch* as in *church* (hard *ch*)
ć/ci	*ci* as in *cappuccino* (soft *ch*)
d	as in *dog*
dz	*ds* as in *odds*
dź/dzi	*j* as in *jeans* (soft *j*)
dż	*j* as in *jaw* (hard *j*)
e	as in *egg*
ę	(nasal *e*) *en* as in *hen* but without the tongue closing on the *n*; before *b* and *p* it sounds more like *em* as in *hemlock*; at the end of a word, it tends to lose its nasal quality and sounds more like the Polish *e*
f	as in *fog*
g	as in *go*
h	as in *hall* (can also be pronounced the same as *ch*)
i	*ee* as in *cheek*

j	*y* as in *yes*
k	as in *key*
l	as in *lamp*
ł	*w* as in *wag*
m	as in *man*
n	as in *not*
ń/ni	*ni* as in *onion* or Spanish *ñ* as in *mañana*
o	as in *hope*
ó	*oo* as in *scoot* (pronounced the same as *u*)
p	as in *pup*
r	*rr* as in Spanish *arriba* (trilled, though not as long as in Spanish)
rz	*s* as in *pleasure* (pronounced the same as *ż*) (hard *zh*)
s	as in *say*
sz	*sh* as in *hush* (hard *sh*)
ś/si	*sh* as in *sheep* (soft *sh*)
t	as in *top*
u	*oo* as in *scoot* (pronounced the same as *ó*)
w	*v* as in *vat*
y	as in *myth*
z	as in *zoo*
ź/zi	*ti* as in *equation* (soft *zh*)
ż	*s* as in *pleasure* (pronounced the same as *rz*) (hard *zh*)

Normally, the next-to-the-last syllable is stressed.

GLOSSARY

It is assumed that the reader will already have some basic familiarity with art history, Greek mythology, Catholicism, and the philosophy of Friedrich Nietzsche to render a much more substantial glossary unnecessary.

Balladyna. the heroine of *Balladyna*, a romantic drama in five acts, written by Juliusz Słowacki and first published in Paris in 1839

Beardsley, Aubrey (1872-1898). English illustrator and author

Bhagavad Gita. a sacred Hindu scripture

bhūtas. Sanskrit word for the ghosts of the deceased or disembodied spirits

Black Lake and Eye of the Sea. Czarny Staw and Morskie Oko, two lakes in the Tatra Mountains in southern Poland

Bronowice chest. a type of dowry chest, usually decorated and painted with flowers; most likely an allusion to Wyspiański's 1901 play *The Wedding*, which is set in the village of Bronowice (now part of Krakow)

Głogów. a city in western Poland

Goplana. nymph queen from Słowacki's *Balladyna* who fell in love with Grabiec when she saved him from drowning

Grabiec. a character from Słowacki's *Balladyna*; Balladyna's lover and the object of Goplana's affection

guṇas. Sanskrit word for the three qualities (sattva, rajas, tamas) that make up a person's character

Highlander. an indigenous ethnic group in southern Poland; also known as Góral

Jędrek Cajka. likely a reference to a character from the 1907 novel *Z Tatr* by Stanisław Witkiewicz

Kalinowszczyzna. a residential district in northeastern Lublin

Krakowskie Przedmieście. one of Lublin's main streets

Lajkonik. a Polish folk character with an Orientalist costume consisting of a bearded rider on a horse and ostensibly commemorating an historical Tartar attack

Maestoso. an Italian musical term directing musicians to perform a passage in a stately, majestic manner; the lyrics are from the 1904 Christmas carol "Jezu Chryste, Panie miły"

Manu. the archetypal first man of Hindu mythology

Maryla. a more aristocratic form of the name Marysia

Marysia the Distant. likely a reference to a character from the 1903 novel *Na skalnym Podhalu* by Kazimierz Przerwa-Tetmajer

master. translation of *mistrz*, a term typically used for teachers and those with a master's degree (as is likely the case within the context of this story)

pan. a Polish title of respect for men roughly equivalent to Mister

pani. a Polish title of respect for women roughly equivalent to Mrs. or Ms.

Podhale. Poland's southernmost region at the foothills of the Tatra Mountains; also known as the Polish Highlands

Postumus. possibly an allusion to the friend addressed in Horace's *Odes*, Book II, Song 14

Przybyszewski, Stanisław (1868-1927). Prussian novelist, dramatist, and poet known for his scandalous, libertine lifestyle

Rops, Félicien (1833-1898). Belgian Symbolist artist

Samkhya Yoga. a practice of Hinduism that seeks to transcend dualistic thinking

Sigismund Bell. the largest of the five bells hanging in the Sigismund Tower in Krakow's Wawel Cathedral

Słobódka. a small town currently Слабодка [Slabodka] in northwestern Belarus; in 1921, when Czechowicz worked there as a teacher, the town was part of Poland and had a population of just under 600 people

Tatras. part of the Western Carpathian mountain range that forms the border between Poland and Slovakia

Vedas. religious texts from ancient India

Vistula. the longest river in Poland, which flows through Krakow

Wawel Cathedral. a Roman Catholic cathedral situated on Wawel Hill in Krakow and part of the Wawel Castle complex; it served as the coronation site of Polish monarchs

Wigilia. traditional Christmas Eve supper and vigil

Wiśnicz. a small town near Krakow known since the Middle Ages for its prison and gallows

Włodzimierz Potocki (1789-1812). a count and colonel in the Duchy of Warsaw's horse artillery; a statue of him by Bertel Thorvaldsen is housed in the Trinity Chapel in Krakow's Wawel Cathedral

wolf of Gubbio. a particularly fierce wolf that was, according to the hagiography, tamed by Francis of Assisi

Wyspiański, Stanisław (1869-1907). a multifaceted artist known for his plays, paintings, and poetry; he designed the stained-glass windows for the apse of Krakow's Franciscan Church

Żmurko, Franciszek (1859-1910). Polish realist painter

TRANSLATOR'S NOTE

We appear suddenly, young and different from you,
amidst the bazar's bustle of merchants, Pharisees,
hucksters — a throng of wild mustangs without bits
or bridles.

    We are not bringing you inspiring ideals (these
have long since been laid to rest in the junk room of
the past) or pronouncements from the Übermensch.

    The solar with our own sun, the floral only
with flowers from our own soul, we toss bunches of
them because toss we must.

    Without a banner with an image of Saint Ism,
without slogans (these are useless to us), flung
together, free sons of Beauty, we wander through our
own wastelands.

Thus begins the editorial-cum-manifesto, written by
Konrad Bielski and Wacław Gralewski, that appeared
in June 1923 in the first (unnumbered) issue of the literary and artistic journal *Reflektor*. The journal, whose
name conjures a bright future and could mean searchlight,
floodlight, spotlight, or headlight, was a turning point in
Polish literary history as well as in the cultural history of
Lublin. It introduced a third strain, after Skamander and

Awangarda Krakowska, of the poetic avant-garde into the newly established Second Republic of Poland. After the above-mentioned editorial and a poem entitled "Konie," also by Gralewski, and under a cover drawn by Jan Wydra, Józef Czechowicz made his literary debut with *The Story of the Paper Crown*.

Perhaps the closest we will ever get to experiencing the thrill of *Reflektor*'s lightning flash upon its premiere was waking up in October 2022 to a flood of news alerts announcing a "new" Czechowicz poem. This untitled poem had been written October 14-15, 1922, when Czechowicz was nineteen years old and teaching in what is today Belarus. According to several naive articles in the Polish press, the poet had written it as a kind of declaration of love for a certain "extremely attractive girl" in whose possession it had been preserved. But the poem, written roughly at the same time as *The Story of the Paper Crown*, may of course just as easily be read, particularly in light of the story's themes and subject matter, *otherwise*. My translation of this newly discovered poem, completed exactly a century later, serves as the second epigraph of this volume. Both the story and the poem, in which we can find some of the musicality, wordplay, and alliteration that gesture to the brilliant poetry that is to come, reveal a young poet still in search of his literary voice. It wouldn't be until 1927 with the publication of his first volume of poetry that the poet's mature voice would finally be heard.

The cover of the first unnumbered issue of *Reflektor*, along with the first page of "Opowieść o papierowej koronie", via Wikisource.

One aspect of that voice, and a common literary device found in the writings of the late Young Poland and early interwar periods, involved writing in dialect. In this story, Czechowicz employs the Podhale dialect or gwara podhalańska, the language of the Polish Highlanders, or Górals. Use of the dialect begins in Scene Four, (the first) Section 4, and is predominately spoken by Marysia and Jędrek Cajka, the two characters most identified as Górals, though other characters, especially Saint Francis and Postumus Porco, also resort to gwara when addressing them.

After several months exploring possible ways to convey the dialectical nuances, from resorting to Scottish, Appalachian, or some other comparable "mountain" or "highland" dialect of English or even simply changing the typography, the choice was made to simply translate gwara into standard English. I only retained a hint of dialectical shift by having Francis speak in a King James, or Early Modern, English.

While my translation does not purport to be a critical edition of Czechowicz's story, I have both taken liberties yet also shown considerable restraint when it came to correcting mistakes in the text. My source was the scanned document and transcription on Wikiźródła (pl.wikisource.org), though I did corroborate with the notes from the *Proza* volume edited by Tadeusz Kłak and published by Wydawnictwo UMCS in 2005.

Some of my corrections include typographical and transcription errors, missing or wrong punctuation, a wrong gender-inflected ending of a past-tense verb, certain inconsistencies in the spelling of names, and the cautious elimination of a handful of the countless (though in all actuality: 428) ellipses. (Czechowicz had used ellipses to set off spoken dialog as well as for other functions; if it was in the least bit obvious, I exchanged those ellipses for quotation marks.) I also made what I think were judicious adjustments in order to limit what I considered an inordinate amount of ableist language while conserving the text's semantic subtleties. Though perhaps not a very controversial emendation, I decided not to add what seemed to be missing section titles (Scene Five and Scene Six), so the subsection numbers of Scene Four repeat.

One particularly curious error in the manuscript was the word *dziecieństwo* from the section Friends, which without the second *e* would simply mean childhood [*dzieciństwo*]. The word *cień*, however, which means shadow, appears to replace the second syllable, so that we have some form that, if it were an actual word, might mean something along the lines of *the shadow of childhood* or more abstractly *children's shadow-dom*. There seems to be no textual reason for such a neologism here, particularly since the character of Madonna Maria (about whose childhood we are reading) does not justify preserving such a mistake no matter how generative it may appear to be.

To thankfully counterbalance these kinds of textual errors that only lead to an impasse is the pure thrill, after slogging through a day of difficult translation, of coming across a sentence such as "Każda ziemia własnym winna kwitnąć kwiatem." Even without a reading knowledge of Polish, it should be easy to see the repeated letter clusters or imagine the tongue-twisting phonemes. Here is but one example of Czechowicz's alliterative mastery in embryonic form. My imperfect solution: "Each field should flourish with its own flowers."

So as not to be remiss, we should address Czechowicz's at times seemingly chaotic verb tenses, which I for the most part maintained. Throughout *The Story of the Paper Crown*, the narrative's chronology abruptly shifts between present and past tenses, sometimes within a single sentence or phrase. Now, having repeatedly read this text over the past few years, I find that there is a kind of jostling, hesitant immediacy that comes through because of the sudden jolts, almost as if an experience and the consciousness of that experience are in a continual struggle without ever collapsing into a pure amorphous timelessness. These kinds of chronological disruptions will eventually, especially in his poetry of the mid-1930s, lead to a general withdrawal from chronology itself. Of these later poems, critic Bogdana Carpenter writes in her 1983 *The Poetic Avant-Garde in Poland, 1918-1939* the following:

> The terror permeating Czechowicz's poetry was connected above all with the slow but irreversible passage of time. For Czechowicz, time was hostile, whether it was the ordinary time of the clock moving slowly by small bits … or the rushing destructive time of the apocalypse…. Time measured by the clock was hateful because it moved in only one direction, the direction of death, but the confusion of time was even more terrifying because it meant final apocalypse, a whirlpool in which everything would perish…. Annihilation of time meant the annihilation of all dimensions, an end to the

objects and beings whose identity depends on clear
lines and division, whether spatial or temporal.

Considering that his writing was headed in this direction,
I felt it prudent to not alter in any significant way his idio-
syncratic use of time and tense here in its earliest, and
possibly roughest and most rudimentary form.

Finally, perhaps the most glaring textual error of all,
however, was the fact that in 1923 *The Story of the Paper
Crown* was published without its author's name. Whether
because of carelessness or strategy, we will never know. As a
translator, though, it is a distinct honor to correct that spe-
cific oversight (or slight or tactic) as well as to provide the
first English translation of this amazing, unreservedly queer,
difficult, unruly story, even if it is a hundred years overdue.

Thank you for reading.

Frank Garrett, PhD
Dallas, Texas

ACKNOWLEDGEMENTS

This project would have been much more difficult, if not impossible, without the generous support, assistance, and camaraderie from the following people: James J. Conway, Stephen Harding, George B. Henson, Paweł Próchniak, Wiola Próchniak, Joshua Rothes and the Sublunary Editions editors, Fernando Sdrigotti, Raya Shapiro, Jacob Siefring, Matthew Spencer, Jola Zandecki, my colleagues at *minor literature[s]*, the participants in my monthly philosophy study group, and countless Polish language teachers and friends over the years. With special thanks to the teams at Green Oaks Physical Therapy and CoreHealth Wellness.

I dedicate this project to everyone who continues to work against Poland's—the current Polish government's— ideology of hatred and to all the great queer Polish artists throughout history.

Jedynym prawem jest miłość, a bez miłości nie ma sprawiedliwości.

ABOUT THE AUTHOR

Much of the brief life of **Józef Czechowicz** orbits around the town of Lublin in southeastern Poland, where he was born 15 March 1903. His childhood was marked by poverty, illness, the threat of war, and the death of his father. In 1920 he volunteered to serve in the Polish Army during the Polish-Soviet War. After his military service and the completion of his studies, he worked as a teacher in rural Poland.

Czechowicz made his literary debut in 1923 with his novella *The Story of the Paper Crown*. In 1927 his first volume of poetry *Kamień* [*Stone*] was published. In the following years, he published seven more volumes of poetry. In the early 1930s after a brief stay in France, Czechowicz relocated to Warsaw, where he lived until the outbreak of World War II. In 1939, he was evacuated to Lublin, where he was killed by a bomb dropped by the German Luftwaffe in an air raid on 9 September. He was thirty-six years old.

Józef Czechowicz, who lived openly as a homosexual, is still considered one of the greatest Polish poets of the twentieth century and one of the main proponents of the literary avant-garde. His writing weaves together nostalgic provincialism, an openness regarding sexuality, prophetically catastrophic visions, folklore and mythology, and technological alienation.

ABOUT THE TRANSLATOR

FRANK GARRETT trained as a translator at the Rainer Schulte Center for Translation Studies at the University of Texas at Dallas and at Philipps-Universität Marburg after earning advanced certification in Polish philology from the Catholic University of Lublin. In 2000 he was a FLAS fellow at the Ivan Franko National University of Lviv, and in 2001 he was a Fulbright scholar in Warsaw. Since 2021 he has served as essays and features editor at *minor literature[s]*. Sublunary Editions published his translation of Bruno Schulz's *Undula* in 2020. Frank lives in Dallas with his husband.

SUBLUNARY EDITIONS is a small, independent press based out of Seattle, Washington, publishing in the field of contemporaneous literature, i.e. writing unbounded by era or geography. A selection of our titles can be found below. You can learn more about us at sublunaryeditions.com

THE CENTAUR TREE / Ilarie Voronca, tr. Christina Tudor-Sideri

THE BOOK OF CONVERSATIONS WITH DAVID EDGAR / Henry Miller

THREE DREAMS / Jean Paul & Laurence Sterne

VAGARIES MALICIEUX / Djuna Barnes

THE LAST DAYS OF IMMANUEL KANT / Thomas De Quincey

MARIA WUTZ / Jean Paul

IF YOU HAD THREE HUSBANDS / Gertrude Stein

FANTASTICKS / Nicholas Breton

IVAN MOSCOW / Boris Pilnyak

POEMS / Karl Kraus

NEWTON'S BRAIN / Jakub Arbes

A LOOKING GLASSE FOR THE COURT / Antonio de Guevara

A CYPRESSE GROVE / WIlliam Drummond of Hawthornden

MORNING STAR / Ada Negri

ZORRILLA, THE POET / José Zorrilla

POEMS / Miguel de Unamuno

ESSAYS, PARADOXES, SOLILOQUIES / Miguel de Unamuno

JOAN OF ARC / Jules Michelet and Thomas De Quincey

PAGES FROM THE DIARY OF A JACKASS / Ante Dukić

PREFACES / Jean Paul

THE CITY OF DREADFUL NIGHT AND OTHER WRITINGS / James Thomson

THE COLLECTED WORKS / Kathleen Tankersley Young

EXERCISES / Benajmín Jarnés

AT THE DOORS AND OTHER STORIES / Boris Pilnyak

SONNETS AND POEMS / Antero de Quental

GEBIR / Walter Savage Landor

HALLUCINATED CITY / Mário de Andrade

THE COLLECTED WORKS / Emanuel Carnevali

TWO STORIES / Jean Paul

BIOGRAPHICAL RECREATIONS FROM THE CRANIUM OF A GIANTESS / Jean Paul

THE COLLECTED POEMS / Amy Levy

FOUR SERMONS / Jeremy Taylor

TENTACULAR CITIES / Émile Verhaeren

LIFE OF DON QUIXOTE AND SANCHO / Miguel de Unamuno

I HAVE SEEN MONSTERS AND ANGELS / Eugene Jolas

SECESSION IN ASTROPOLIS / Eugene Jolas